Mother Goose
AND FRIENDS

selected and illustrated by
Ruth Sanderson

 LITTLE, BROWN AND COMPANY
New York ↠ Boston

Little, Brown and Company

Hachette Book Group USA
237 Park Avenue, New York, NY 10017
Visit our Web site at www.lb-kids.com

First Edition: March 2008

Library of Congress Cataloging-in-Publication Data

Mother Goose and friends.
     Mother Goose and friends / selected and illustrated by Ruth Sanderson.
          p. cm.
Summary: A collection of traditional nursery rhymes, including such familiar verses as "Jack and
Jill," "Baa, Baa, Black Sheep," "Little Boy Blue," "Old King Cole," "Wee
Willie Winkie," "Twinkle, Twinkle, Little Star," and many more.
ISBN-13: 978-0-316-77718-6
ISBN-10: 0-316-77718-8
 1. Nursery rhymes. 2. Children's poetry. [1. Nursery rhymes.] I. Sanderson, Ruth. II. Title.

PZ8.3 .M85 2003
398.8—dc21

                                                                                        2001050544

10 9 8 7 6 5 4 3 2

TWP

Printed in Singapore

The illustrations for this book were done in oils on Giverny paper, watercolor paper,
and hardboard panel.
The text was set in Nordik, and the display type is Copperplate.

To Jane Yolen,
a modern-day Mother Goose

INTRODUCTION

Nursery rhymes have existed for as long as mothers have been rocking their children to sleep. The origins of these songs, lullabies, rhymes, and nonsense verses are debated but largely unknown. They first appeared in print in the late eighteenth century in England under the title *Mother Goose's Melodies*, with fifty-one rhymes in all. Soon after came the first U.S. edition, and since then countless illustrated versions have been produced, with many verses added and subtracted over the years. Children today still love these silly, magical, and sometimes mysterious rhymes. Repeating the verses makes learning to speak a great game, and parents take delight when their two- or three-year-old recites— or even sings—the rhymes to them word for word.

In this volume you will find many familiar friends such as Little Bo-Peep, Humpty Dumpty, and Wee Willie Winkie, but I have also introduced some new faces who I hope will become new friends, including The Purple Cow, The Elf-Man, and The Grasshopper. During my research, I fell in love with a few rhymes from the turn of the twentieth century that are not from the traditional Mother Goose "lexicon," but I knew that children would find their singsong quality and whimsical subject matter as irresistible as I did. When the author is known, credit is given under the rhyme.

The challenge for any artist illustrating a Mother Goose collection is to create pictures that are as much fun to look at as the verses are to hear. My goal was to render a world that felt believable and real even though the subject matter is often fanciful. I love to paint nature, so I have set many of the pictures in woods, fields, and gardens. A number of Mother Goose's shy little fairy friends have come out of hiding and appear from time to time in the art, sometimes in starring roles. (I am convinced that anyone who rides on a gander must be friendly with the wee folk!)

Most of the illustrations in this book were done in oils on primed watercolor paper, with a few of the large ones painted on gessoed board. Each one took from one to three weeks to complete. Before I began to paint, however, there was an enormous amount of preliminary work to do.

After looking over many volumes of nursery rhymes, I selected my personal favorites and the ones that I felt had the most child appeal. Then I created small "thumbnail" sketches of each rhyme, and after that a rough full-size book dummy with the text pasted in place. Next I found models for the characters and spent several weeks photographing them in improvised costumes. (I even found a large stuffed goose with its wings outstretched, which was a big help for painting the goose's detailed feathers.) The next step was to create another book dummy with finished pencil sketches. And finally I painted the illustrations. I worked on three or more pieces at a time, alternating days between them, so I always had a fresh eye for the work.

I hope you will enjoy reading this book with a special child. And if my pictures add some pleasure to the experience, then the three years that I worked to create the art will have been time well spent.

Ruth Sanderson

OLD MOTHER GOOSE

Old Mother Goose,
When she wanted to wander,
Would ride through the air
On a very fine gander.
Mother Goose had a house,
'Twas built in a wood,
Where an owl at the door
For a sentinel stood.

THERE WAS AN OLD WOMAN

There was an old woman
Who lived in a shoe.
She had so many children,
She didn't know what to do.
She gave them some broth
With plenty of bread.
She kissed them all sweetly
And put them to bed.

PETER, PETER, PUMPKIN-EATER

Peter, Peter, pumpkin-eater,
Had a wife and couldn't keep her.
So he put her in a pumpkin shell,
And there he kept her very well.

9

PUSSYCAT, PUSSYCAT

"Pussycat, Pussycat,
Where have you been?"
"I've been to London
To visit the queen."
"Pussycat, Pussycat,
What did you there?"
"I frightened a little mouse
Under her chair."

10

LAVENDER'S BLUE

Lavender's blue, dilly, dilly,
Rosemary's green.
When I am king, dilly, dilly,
You shall be queen!

THIS LITTLE PIG

This little pig went to market,

This little pig stayed home,

This little pig had roast beef,

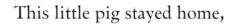

This little pig had none,

This little pig cried, "Wee, wee, wee!"
All the way home.

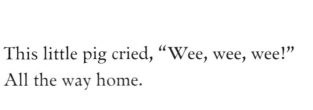

THREE LITTLE KITTENS

Three little kittens
Lost their mittens,
And they began to cry,
"Oh, Mother dear,
We sadly fear,
Our mittens we have lost."
"What! Lost your mittens,
You naughty kittens,
Then you shall have no pie."

Three little kittens
Found their mittens,
And they began to cry,
"Oh, Mother dear,
See here, see here,
Our mittens we have found."
"What! Found your mittens,
You darling kittens,
Now you shall have some pie."

HUMPTY DUMPTY

Humpty Dumpty sat on the wall.
Humpty Dumpty had a great fall.
All the king's horses and all the king's men
Couldn't put Humpty together again.

14

THE QUEEN OF HEARTS

The Queen of Hearts,
She made some tarts
All on a summer's day;
The Knave of Hearts,
He stole the tarts
And took them clean away.

15

GRAY GOOSE AND GANDER

Gray goose and gander,
Waft your wings together,
And carry the good king's daughter
Over the one-strand river.

16

MARY HAD A LITTLE LAMB

Mary had a little lamb
With fleece as white as snow,
And everywhere that Mary went
The lamb was sure to go.

It followed her to school one day,
That was against the rule;
It made the children laugh and play
To see a lamb at school.

17

THE OWL

Of all the gay birds that e'er I did see,
The owl is the fairest by far to me;
For all the day long she sits on a tree,
And when the night comes, away flies she.

TWO LITTLE BLACKBIRDS

Two little blackbirds
Sitting on a hill—
One named Jack,
The other named Jill.
Fly away, Jack,
Fly away, Jill.
Come back, Jack,
Come back, Jill.

18

PIT, PAT, WELL-A-DAY

Pit, pat, well-a-day,
Little robin flew away.
Where can little robin be?
Gone into the cherry tree.

MARCH WINDS

March winds and April showers
Bring forth May flowers.

SING A SONG OF SIXPENCE

Sing a song of sixpence,
A pocket full of rye;
Four-and-twenty blackbirds
Baked in a pie.

When the pie was opened,
The birds began to sing;
Was not that a dainty dish
To set before the king?

The king was in his countinghouse,
Counting out his money;
The queen was in the parlor,
Eating bread and honey.

The maid was in the garden,
Hanging out the clothes;
Down came a blackbird,
And pecked at her nose.

PEASE PORRIDGE HOT

Pease porridge hot,
Pease porridge cold,
Pease porridge in the pot,
Nine days old.
Some like it hot,
Some like it cold,
Some like it in the pot,
Nine days old.

JACK SPRAT

Jack Sprat could eat no fat,
His wife could eat no lean.
And so, betwixt them both, you see,
They licked the platter clean.

OLD KING COLE

Old King Cole was a merry old soul,
And a merry old soul was he.
He called for his pipe,
And he called for his bowl,
And he called for his fiddlers three.

DOODLE DOODLE DOO

Doodle doodle doo,
The princess lost her shoe.
Her highness hopped,
The fiddler stopped,
Not knowing what to do.

THE MUFFIN MAN

"Oh, do you know the muffin man,
The muffin man, the muffin man,
Oh, do you know the muffin man
Who lives on Drury Lane?"

"Oh, yes, I know the muffin man,
The muffin man, the muffin man,
Oh, yes, I know the muffin man
Who lives on Drury Lane."

PETER PIPER

Peter Piper picked
A peck of pickled peppers;
A peck of pickled peppers
Peter Piper picked.
If Peter Piper picked
A peck of pickled peppers,
Where's the peck of pickled peppers
Peter Piper picked?

LITTLE MISS MUFFET

Little Miss Muffet
Sat on a tuffet,
Eating her curds and whey;
Along came a spider,
Who sat down beside her
And frightened Miss Muffet away.

POLLY, PUT THE KETTLE ON

Polly, put the kettle on,
Polly, put the kettle on,
Polly, put the kettle on,
And let's drink tea.

Sukey, take it off again,
Sukey, take it off again,
Sukey, take it off again,
They've all gone away.

28

THE CAT TEA PARTY

What did she see,
Oh, what did she see?
Why, all the cats had come to tea.
Dear me, oh, dear me—
She didn't know
If bread and butter they'd like or no.
They might want little mice, oh! oh!
Dear me, oh, dear me—
Why, all the cats had come to tea.

OLD WOMAN

There was an old woman
Lived under a hill,
And if she's not gone,
She lives there still.

30

THERE WAS A CROOKED MAN

There was a crooked man,
And he went a crooked mile,
And he found a crooked sixpence
Against a crooked stile;
He bought a crooked cat,
Which caught a crooked mouse,
And they all lived together
In a little crooked house.

CACKLE, CACKLE

Cackle, cackle, Madam Goose,
Have you any feathers loose?
Truly have I, little fellow,
Half enough to fill a pillow.
Here are quills, take one or two,
And down to make a bed for you.

WHERE HAS MY LITTLE DOG GONE?

Oh where, oh where has my little dog gone?
Oh where, oh where can he be?
With his ears cut short and his tail cut long,
Oh where, oh where can he be?

I LIKE LITTLE PUSSY

I like little pussy,
Her coat is so warm,
And if I don't hurt her,
She'll do me no harm.
So I'll not pull her tail,
Nor drive her away,
But pussy and I
Very gently will play.

33

HERE WE GO ROUND

Here we go round the mulberry bush,
The mulberry bush, the mulberry bush,
Here we go round the mulberry bush,
So early in the morning.

RING AROUND THE ROSIES

Ring around the rosies,
A pocketful of posies,
Ashes, ashes,
We all fall down.

SEESAW, MARGERY DAW

Seesaw, Margery Daw,
Johnny shall have a new master.
He shall have but a penny a day,
Because he can't work any faster.

HICKETY, PICKETY

Hickety, pickety, my black hen,
She lays eggs for gentlemen;
Sometimes nine
And sometimes ten;
Hickety, pickety, my black hen.

YANKEE DOODLE

Yankee Doodle went to town
Riding on a pony,
Stuck a feather in his hat
And called it macaroni.

MARY, MARY, QUITE CONTRARY

Mary, Mary, quite contrary,
How does your garden grow?
Silver bells and cockleshells
And pretty maids all in a row.

LITTLE BOY BLUE

Little Boy Blue, come blow your horn;
The sheep's in the meadow, the cow's in the corn.
Where's the little boy who looks after the sheep?
He's under the haystack, fast asleep.
Will you wake him? No, not I;
For if I do, he'll be sure to cry.

LITTLE BO-PEEP

Little Bo-Peep has lost her sheep
And can't tell where to find them;
Leave them alone, and they'll come home,
Wagging their tails behind them.

BAA, BAA, BLACK SHEEP

Baa, baa, black sheep,
Have you any wool?
Yes, sir, yes, sir,
Three bags full;
One for the master,
One for the dame,
And one for the little boy
Who lives down the lane.

40

JACK AND JILL

Jack and Jill went up the hill
To fetch a pail of water;
Jack fell down and broke his crown,
And Jill came tumbling after.

LONDON BRIDGE

London Bridge is falling down,
Falling down, falling down.
London Bridge is falling down,
My fair lady.

HANDY SPANDY

Handy Spandy, Jack-a-Dandy,
Loved plum cake and sugar candy.
He bought some at a grocer's shop,
And out he came—hop, hop, hop.

SEESAW, SACARADOWN

Seesaw, sacaradown, sacaradown,
Which is the way to London town?
One foot up, and the other foot down,
That is the way to London town.

THE GRASSHOPPER

The Grasshopper, the Grasshopper,
I will explain to you—
He is the Brownies' racehorse
And the fairies' Kangaroo!

—Vachel Lindsey

43

RIDE A COCKHORSE

Ride a cockhorse to Banbury Cross,
To see a fine lady upon a white horse;
With rings on her fingers and bells on her toes,
She shall have music wherever she goes.

CLOUDS

White sheep, white sheep,
On a blue hill,
When the wind stops,
You all stand still.
When the wind blows,
You walk away slow.
White sheep, white sheep,
Where do you go?

CATKIN

I have a little pussy
And her coat is silver-gray;
She lives in a wide meadow
And she never runs away.
She'll always be a pussy,
She'll never be a cat,
Because—she's a pussy willow!
Now what do you think of that?

HICKORY, DICKORY, DOCK

Hickory, dickory, dock,
The mouse ran up the clock!
The clock struck one,
And down he ran,
Hickory, dickory, dock.

LITTLE JACK HORNER

Little Jack Horner sat in a corner,
Eating a Christmas pie.
He put in his thumb
And pulled out a plum
And said, "What a good boy am I!"

DEEDLE, DEEDLE

Deedle, deedle, dumpling, my son John
Went to bed with his stockings on;
One shoe off, and one shoe on,
Deedle, deedle, dumpling, my son John.

JACK BE NIMBLE

Jack be nimble, Jack be quick,
Jack jump over the candlestick.

SEVEN BLACKBIRDS IN A TREE

Seven blackbirds in a tree,
Count them and see what they be.
One for sorrow,
Two for joy,
Three for a girl,
Four for a boy;
Five for silver,
Six for gold,
Seven for a secret
That's never been told.

50

DANCE, LITTLE BABY

Dance, little baby, dance up high!
Never mind, baby, mother is by.
Crow and caper, caper and crow;
There, little baby, there you go!
Up to the ceiling and down to the ground,
Backward and forward, round and round;
Dance, little baby, and mother will sing,
With the merry chorus, ding, ding, ding!

51

THE CAT AND THE FIDDLE

Hey, diddle, diddle!
The cat and the fiddle,
The cow jumped over the moon;
The little dog laughed
To see such sport,
And the dish ran away with the spoon.

THE ELF-MAN

I met a little Elf-Man once,
Down where the lilies blow.
I asked him why he was so small
And why he didn't grow.

He slightly frowned, and with his eye
He looked me through and through.
"I'm quite as big for me," he said,
"As you are big for you."

—John Kendrick Bangs

53

LITTLE ROBIN RED-BREAST

Little Robin Red-Breast
Sat upon a rail;
Needle, naddle went his head,
Wiggle, waggle went his tail.

THE PURPLE COW

I never saw a purple cow;
I never hope to see one.
But I can tell you, anyhow,
I'd rather see than be one.

—Gelett Burgess

WHO EVER SAW A RABBIT?

Who ever saw a rabbit
Dressed in a riding habit
Gallop off to see her friends, in this style?
I would not be surprised
If the lady is capsized
Before she has ridden half a mile.

54

DONKEY, DONKEY

Donkey, donkey, old and gray,
Open your mouth and gently bray;
Lift your ears and blow your horn
To wake the world this sleepy morn.

TO MARKET, TO MARKET

To market, to market, to buy a fat pig;
Home again, home again, jiggety jig.
To market, to market, to buy a fat hog;
Home again, home again, jiggety jog.

MARY HAD A PRETTY BIRD

Mary had a pretty bird,
Feathers bright and yellow;
Slender legs, upon my word,
He was a pretty fellow.
The sweetest notes he always sang,
Which quite delighted Mary;
And near the cage she'd always sit
To hear her own canary.

TWINKLE, TWINKLE, LITTLE STAR

Twinkle, twinkle, little star,
How I wonder what you are;
Up above the world so high,
Like a diamond in the sky,
Twinkle, twinkle, little star;
How I wonder what you are.

HUSH, LITTLE BABY

Hush, little baby, don't say a word;
Papa's gonna buy you a mockingbird.
And if that mockingbird don't sing,
Papa's gonna buy you a diamond ring.
And if that diamond ring turns brass,
Papa's gonna buy you a looking glass.
And if that looking glass gets broke,
Papa's gonna buy you a billy goat.
And if that billy goat runs away,
Papa's gonna buy you another someday.

SLEEP, BABY, SLEEP

Sleep, baby, sleep,
Down where the woodbines creep;
Be always like the lamb so mild,
A kind and sweet and gentle child.
Sleep, baby, sleep.

WEE WILLIE WINKIE

Wee Willie Winkie
Runs through the town,
Upstairs and downstairs,
In his nightgown;
Rapping at the window,
Crying at the lock,
"Are the children in their beds?
For now it's eight o'clock."

BEDTIME

The Man in the Moon looked out of the moon,
Looked out of the moon and said,
"'Tis time for all children upon the earth
To think about getting to bed!"

STAR LIGHT, STAR BRIGHT

Star light, star bright,
First star I see tonight.
I wish I may, I wish I might,
Have the wish I wish tonight.

INDEX